TABLE OF CONTENTS

Years ago in a distant galaxy, the planet Krypton exploded. Its only survivor was a baby named Kal-El who escaped in a rocket ship. After landing on Earth, he was adopted by the Kents, a kind couple who named him Clark. The boy soon discovered he had extraordinary abilities fueled by the yellow sun of Earth. He chose to use these powers to help others, and so he became the guardian of his new home.

He is . . .

SUPERMAN™

CHAPTER 1

A Call for Help

Danny Wilkes was already running late for work. Wearing his sharply pressed suit, he dodged traffic as he crossed the busy street. Once at his car, he fumbled through his pocket for his keys. He carefully balanced the cardboard tray of coffee cups he carried as he quickly unlocked his door. Danny sighed with relief as he slid into the driver's seat and shut the door behind him. He might not be late after all.

The car door swung back open.

"What in the world?" Danny asked as he closed the door again. It swung open again—all by itself.

As Danny reached for the door handle, the car seat bucked beneath him. "Hey!" he shouted as it tossed him out of the car.

THUNK! SPLOOSH!

Danny landed on the hard pavement under a shower of hot coffee.

"Hey!" repeated someone nearby.

"My word!" said another.

"What's going on?" asked someone else.

Danny's eyes widened as he watched other drivers being hurled from their cars all down the street.

KRASH! KRUNCH! KRASH! KRASH!

One by one, cars lurched forward, smashing into the vehicles in front of them. People scrambled to get clear as their cars created a long, single-file crash. Glass shattered and metal creaked as the vehicles fused together somehow. Then the entire creation rose off the street as if it were alive.

Danny joined the screaming crowd as they ran for safety. It looked as if he wasn't the only one who was going to be late this morning.

* * *

On the other side of Metropolis, Lois Lane stood beside Clark Kent's desk at the *Daily Planet* newspaper office. The reporter was flipping through her notebook as she ran through the last of her notes. She wanted to see if her recent investigation had any ties to Clark's latest news story.

"Well, what do you think, Clark?" Lois frowned when she realized her fellow reporter was no longer listening.

"Hello?" Lois asked. She waved a hand in front of his face. "Earth to Clark."

Clark had only missed her last few sentences. Thanks to his super-hearing, his attention had been on something else—the cries of alarm and sounds of destruction coming from across town.

He shook his head. "I'm sorry, Lois." He sprang to his feet. "I just remembered . . . I have to meet with a source for a new story."

Lois crossed her arms and smirked. "Been holding out on me, Smallville?" She often used Clark's hometown as a nickname.

"Not really." Clark smiled. "This is brand new . . . *really* new."

Clark ducked into the nearby stairwell and sped up the steps. He removed his glasses and loosened his tie as he neared the roof. Clark hadn't actually lied to Lois. From the combination of sounds he had heard, a big news story probably was waiting for him across the city. And, as Superman, he was going right to the source.

WHOOSH!

The roof's door flew open, and a blue and red streak rocketed out. Superman circled the shining globe atop the building before flying toward the emergency. Blurry skyscrapers whizzed by as he sped over the city.

As Superman neared the scene, he spotted plumes of smoke rising up from the destruction. He also saw the long tail of some enormous creature. It disappeared around a building as he approached.

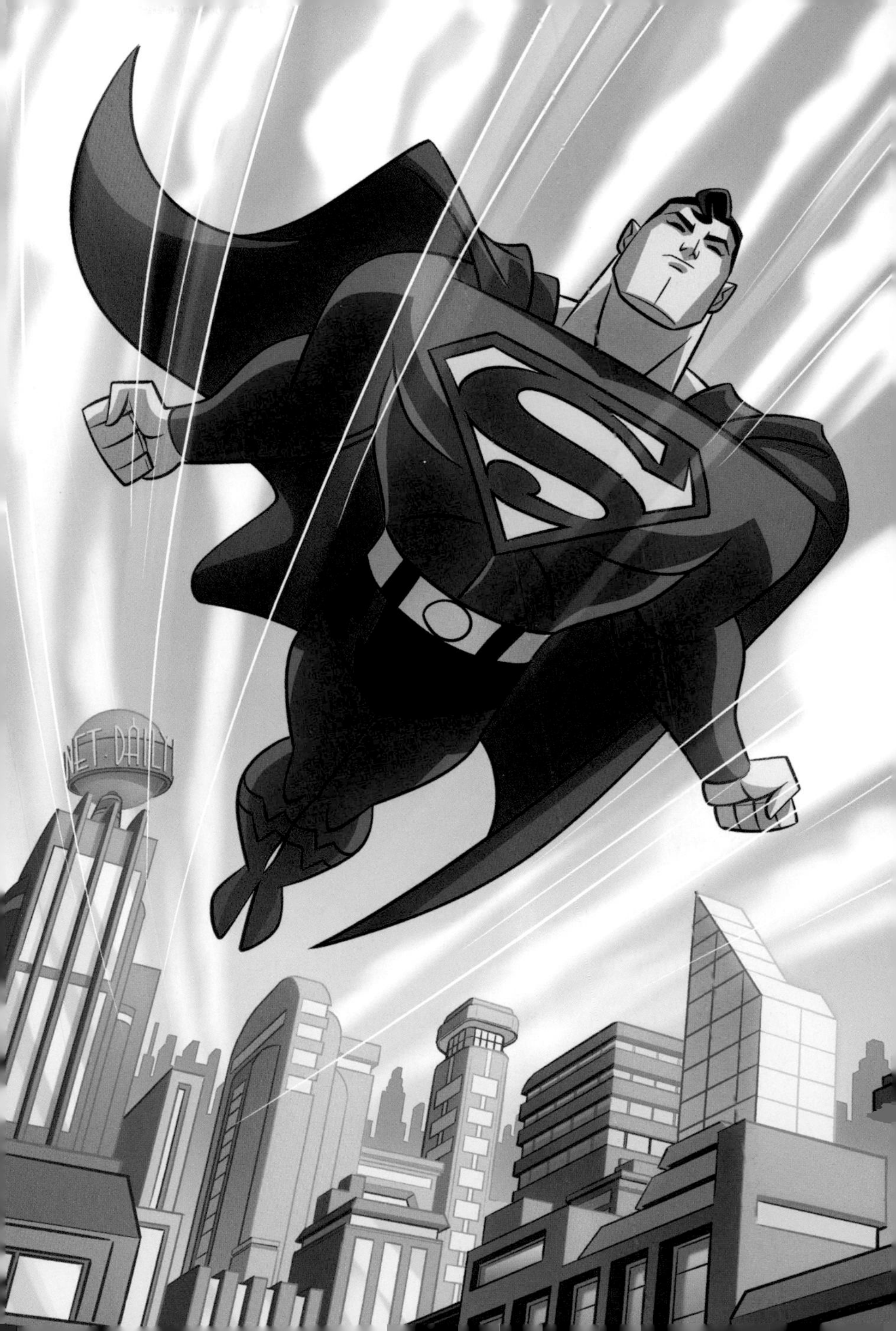
NET·DAILY

What is that? Superman thought.

The Man of Steel raced after the creature. He darted around the corner as the tail was about to disappear behind yet another building.

"Oh, no you don't," Superman said as he grabbed onto the tail. He dug his heels into the pavement, keeping the creature from escaping.

That's when he noticed the long tail was actually made of metal. More than that, it was formed from a bunch of cars fused together.

As Superman held tight, the end of the tail snapped off in his arms. He dropped the piece and scanned the crushed cars with his X-ray vision. Luckily, no one was trapped inside. That's when the strangest thing happened.

KRACK! KREEEEEK! KRUNCH!

The broken piece suddenly reattached itself. The metal creaked and groaned as it joined with the rest of the tail.

"It's time to see what kind of creature this belongs to," he said as he rose off the ground.

Superman didn't have to find the other end of the metallic creature; it came to him. Before he could move, the head of a giant snake appeared around the corner. Its long body of connected cars gathered beneath it as it rose into the air. It looked ready to strike.

Superman balled up his fists, preparing to attack. Unfortunately, the metal snake struck first. With lightning speed, it wrapped him tightly in its coils. Superman struggled to break free as the metal snake brought him closer to its gaping mouth.

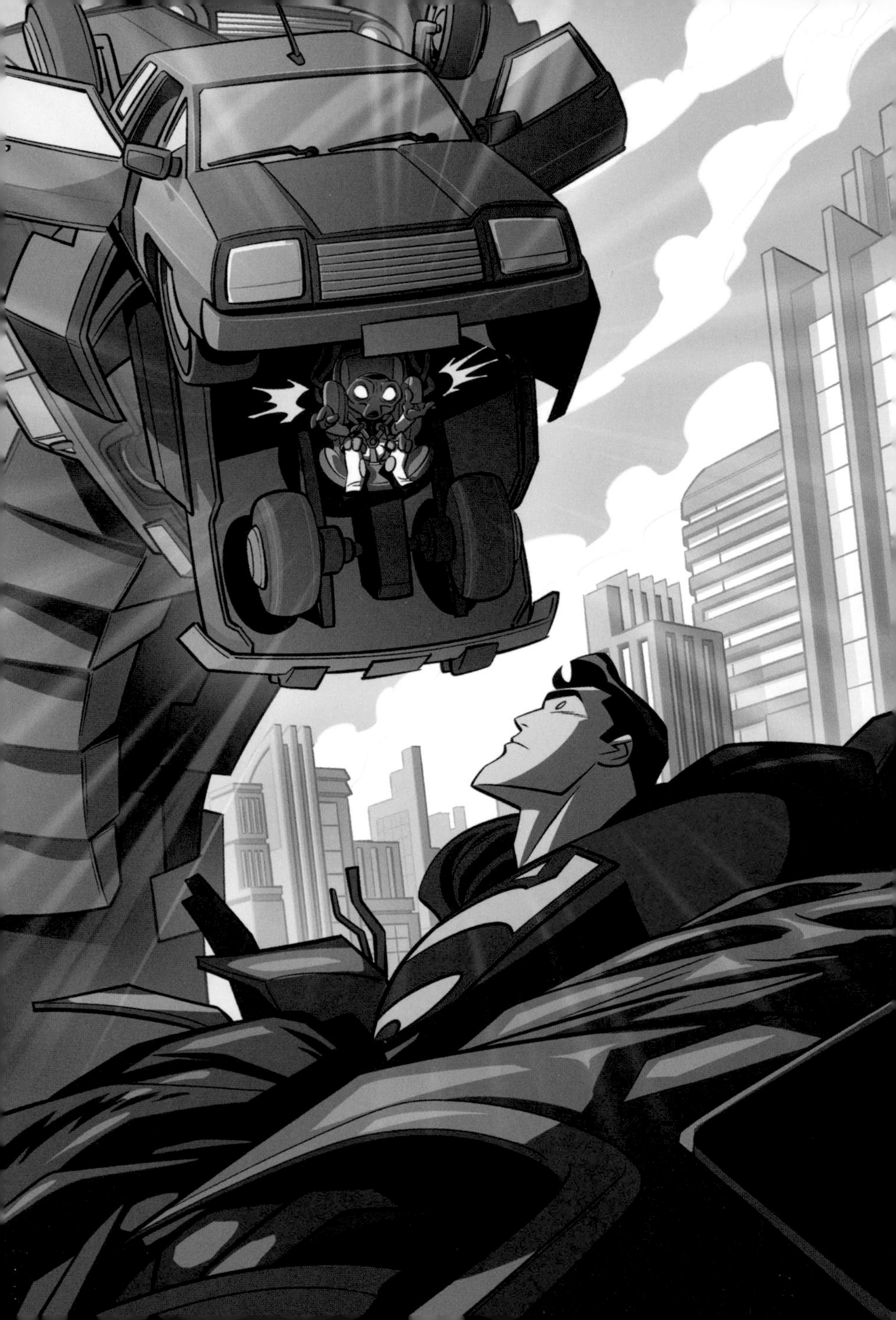

Just when he expected to be swallowed whole, Superman instead saw a small creature inside the snake's mouth. He had glowing eyes, green skin, and four arms. He was so small that he was strapped inside a child's car seat.

"Hello, Superman," the creature said, waving two of its hands. "I'm sorry about the mess. But I had to get your attention somehow."

The coils loosened, and Superman flew free. "Do I know you?"

"My name is Xal Gliknark, from the planet Balvin," the alien said as he unbuckled himself and hopped to the ground. "But most people just call me the Mechanic." He gestured back to the snake. "Because I can control just about any kind of machinery."

"Why did you need my attention?" Superman asked.

"Actually, I need your help!" the tiny alien corrected. The Mechanic nervously rubbed his four hands together. "I'm being hunted, across the galaxy, by the most vile, disgusting creature who ever . . ."

VROOOOOOOOM!

A deep, rolling rumble suddenly filled the air. The sound grew louder as a noisy hoverbike came into view. It swooped down from the sky, leaving a trail of black smoke behind it.

The alien driving the vehicle was dressed in leather and had a chain and hook wrapped around one arm. His chalk-white skin glistened in the sun, and his thick, black hair ruffled in the wind. He pulled to a stop in front of them.

The Man of Steel groaned at the sight of this particular alien. It was Lobo—an intergalactic bounty hunter and general pain in the neck, as far as Superman was concerned.

"Hi-ya, Supes," Lobo said in a deep, gravelly voice. He hopped off the hoverbike and spread his arms wide. "Long time, no see, pal!"

CHAPTER 2

Mechanical Trouble

Superman frowned at the new arrival. "I thought I told you never to return to Earth, Lobo."

"What? You were serious about that?" the bounty hunter asked, eyes wide as if with surprise. He gently placed a hand to his chest. "I'm hurt! Well, don't you worry, I'll just collect my bounty and let you get back to whatever weird super hero business you have going here."

The Mechanic took a couple steps back and hid behind Superman's cape.

"I'm afraid I can't let you do that," the hero said. "The Mechanic is now under my protection."

Lobo moved closer to Superman. "Now you see there . . . *that's* gonna be a problem." The bounty hunter pointed down at the Mechanic. "Because some nice folks are paying me mucho credits to bring this guy in." He jutted a thumb at his own chest. "And I don't have to tell you, the Main Man always delivers."

"Listen, Lobo—" Superman began.

POW! With lightning speed, Lobo lurched forward and punched the Man of Steel. The Mechanic barely jumped clear as Superman flew across the street and slammed into a nearby building.

The hero shook his head as he climbed out of a crater in the side of the marble wall. He had forgotten just how hard Lobo could hit. The bounty hunter was as strong and invincible as he was.

WHOOSH!

Superman pushed off the building and flew toward Lobo. The Man of Steel put Lobo in a bear hug before flying straight up. He carried the bounty hunter high into the clouds.

"Come on, Supes," Lobo said with a chuckle. "Quit playing around."

Lobo puffed out his chest and flexed his arm muscles, breaking Superman's grip. Then he balled his hands together and swung them at the hero with all his might. Superman soared through the clouds while Lobo dropped like a stone.

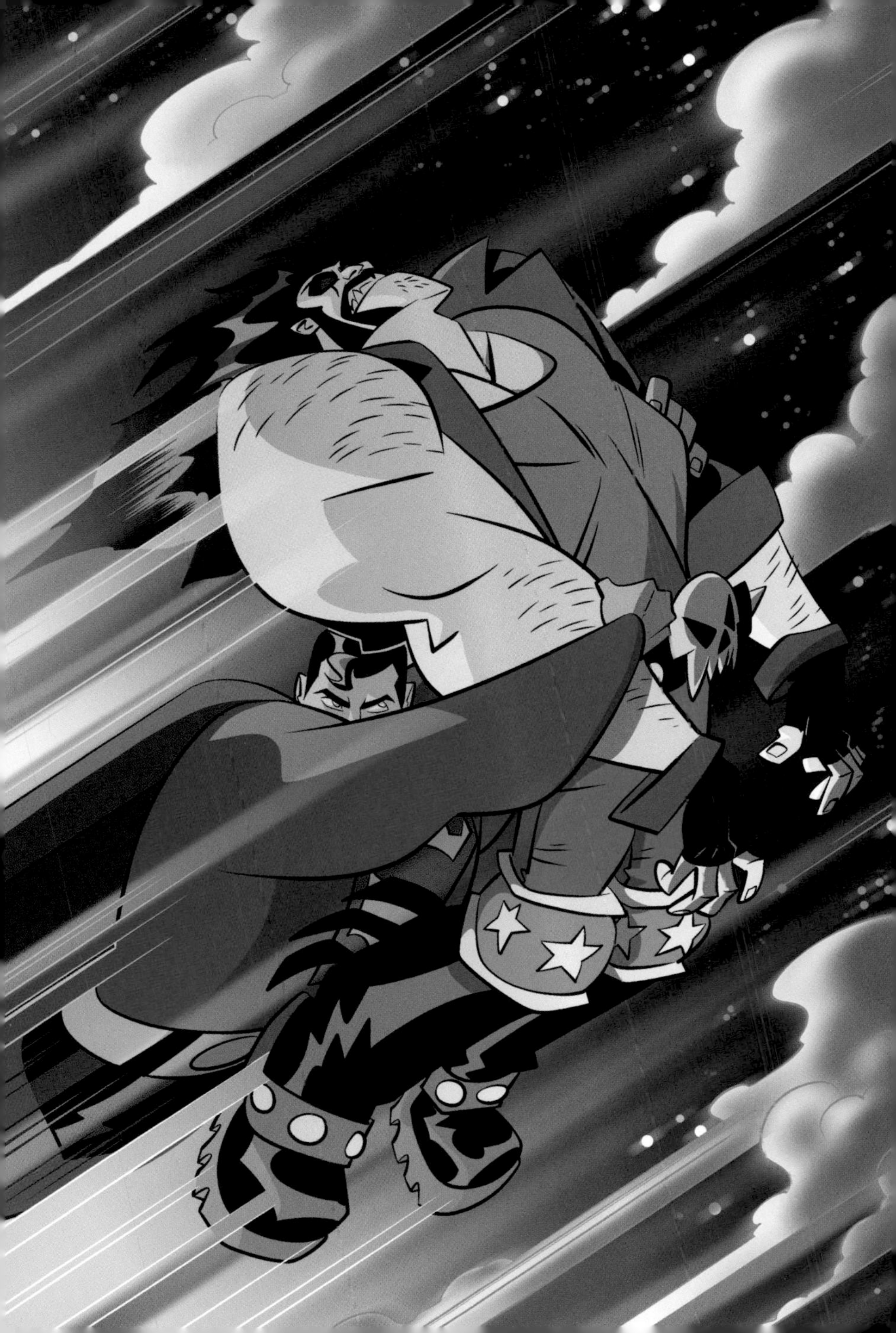

The bounty hunter whistled loudly and his hoverbike flew up to meet him. Lobo plopped onto the seat and revved the engine.

VROOOM! VROOOM!

He aimed the bike toward the Mechanic. "All right, little guy," Lobo growled. "Now that your bodyguard is gone, let's go for a ride."

Lobo sped toward the tiny alien. As he neared, he reached out and prepared to snatch the little guy off the ground. To the bounty hunter's surprise, he was the one grabbed—plucked right off his bike.

"Hey!" Lobo shouted as he tried to wriggle free. He turned to see that the giant car snake held him by the scruff of his leather jacket. He looked down at the alien. The Mechanic's eyes glowed as he glared back up at the bounty hunter.

"Are you doing that?" Lobo asked. "That's a neat trick." The bounty hunter snarled. "I hate neat tricks!"

BAM!

Lobo punched a hole in the head of the car snake, but it didn't release him. Instead, it wrapped the bounty hunter in its massive coils. Metal creaked and Lobo grunted as it squeezed him tighter. "No . . . giant snake is going . . . to crush . . . the Main Man!"

WHOOOSH!

Suddenly, the Mechanic was swooped off the ground.

"Let's get you out of here," Superman said as he flew the alien out of harm's way. "And far away from the city, so no one will get hurt. Maybe then I can talk some sense into Lobo."

"I don't think that's possible," said the Mechanic.

The Man of Steel flew out of the city and across the harbor. Jets of water trailed behind them as they zoomed just above the ocean's surface.

BZZZZZ!

Superman picked up a buzzing sound with his super-hearing. He glanced back just in time to see a missile speeding toward them. The hero banked to one side in the nick of time.

THOOM!

The missile exploded, and the two tumbled toward the sea. The Man of Steel straightened out and flew toward a nearby oil derrick. He set the alien on the deck among many confused crew members.

"Wait here," the hero told him. "I'll take care of Lobo."

"But I can help," said the Mechanic.

Superman smiled at him. "You came to me for help, remember?" He leaped into the sky and zipped toward Lobo.

The bounty hunter fired another missile, but this time, Superman was ready. His eyes narrowed and two thin, red beams shot from them. The beams from his heat vision went straight for the missile.

Ka-THOOM!

Superman flew through the explosion and raced toward the bounty hunter.

Lobo laughed. "Come to Papa!" he yelled before leaping off his hoverbike. He slammed into the super hero and laid into him like a punching bag.

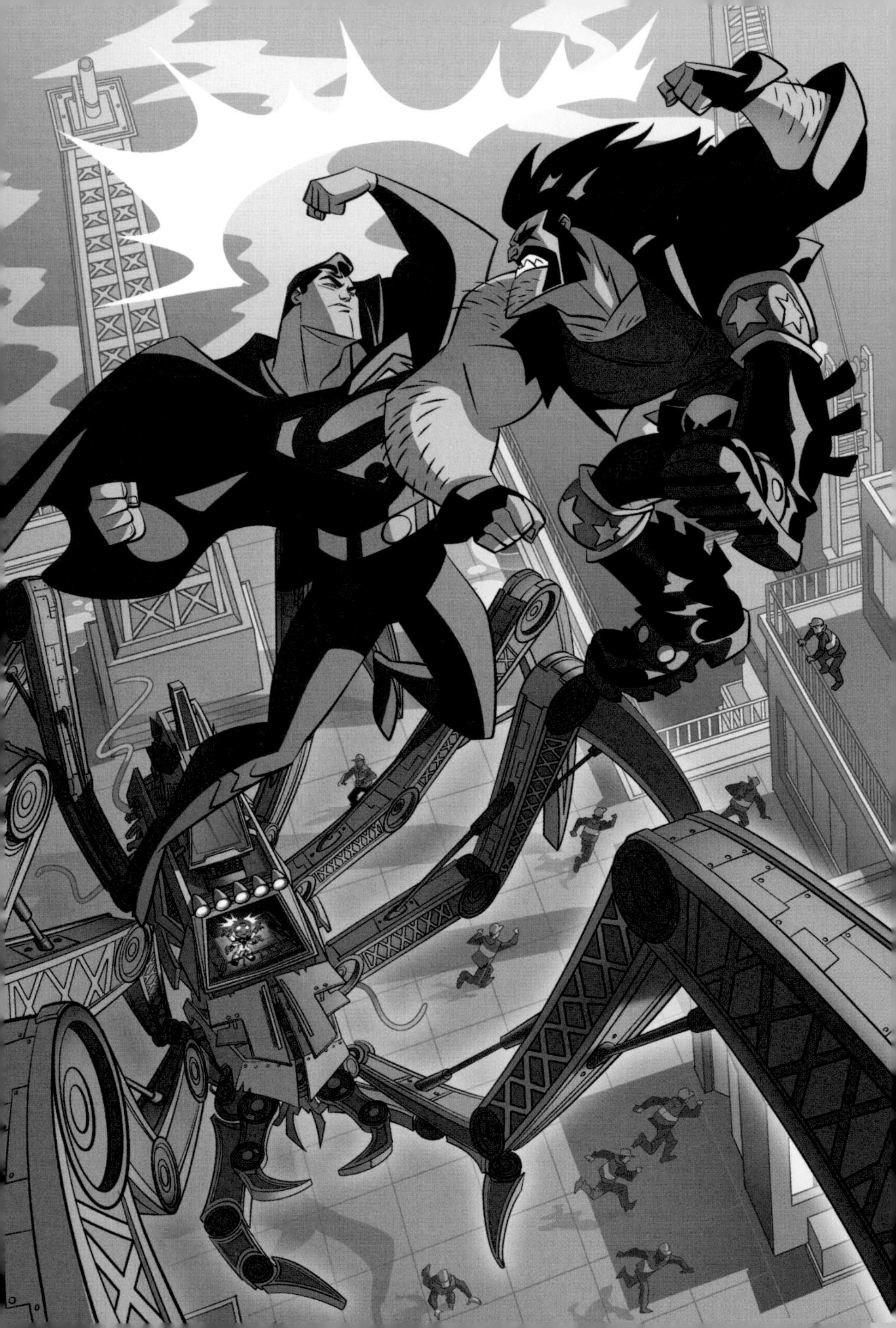

"Let's . . . talk about this," Superman said, between punches.

"Nothing to talk about, Big Blue," Lobo replied. "The little guy is my bounty, and I'm here to collect."

HELP! HELP!

Shouts of alarm caught Superman's attention. Below them, the crew members on the oil derrick leaped into the ocean as the structure came to life. Part of the huge structure walked forward like a giant spider.

What is the Mechanic doing? Superman thought. *Someone's going to get hurt.*

He dropped Lobo and flew to help. He swooped down and grabbed a lifeboat in each hand. He dropped them near the floating crew members and began helping them aboard.

Meanwhile, Lobo dropped onto his hoverbike and hit the gas. The bike roared as he went for the Mechanic.

The bounty hunter laughed as he flew toward the derrick. The spiderlike creature swung at him with long crane arms and drill pipes. The bounty hunter gripped the handlebars of his hoverbike tighter and dodged every attack.

"I've taken on Anderian thorn spiders bigger than this," Lobo said with a laugh. "This is nothing!" He loosened the chain and hook from around his arm.

WHOOP-WHOOP-WHOOP-WHOOP!

Lobo swung the chain over his head as he approached the Mechanic. The little alien's eyes glowed brighter as he controlled the derrick's movements. He made the rig shoot a jet of oil at the approaching bounty hunter.

Lobo dipped his bike and easily flew under the black stream. Then he zipped close and wrapped the chain around the Mechanic's body. He snatched him out of the mechanical spider and flew up to the clouds.

With the alien gone, the oil derrick returned to normal. As Superman placed two crew members into a lifeboat, he saw Lobo and the Mechanic getting away.

Superman sighed. "Dealing with Lobo can never be simple."

CHAPTER 3

No Holding Back

Earth shrank behind them as Lobo and the Mechanic rocketed through space. The bounty hunter gripped the handlebars of his hoverbike while the short alien rode on the seat behind him. The Mechanic was wrapped up in Lobo's chain, to keep him in place.

"I don't understand why you are doing this!" the Mechanic said. "Where are you taking me?"

Lobo let out a deep laugh. "You'll find out soon enough."

VROOM! VROOM!

The bounty hunter revved the throttle, increasing their speed. Within seconds they shot past the Moon.

"And if you don't give me any more trouble, I'll let you stay awake for the ride." Lobo turned and grinned at him. "Because if I see one more monster snake or giant spider-thing, it's a bop on the head and lights out for you."

As Lobo faced front once more, the Mechanic's eyes began to glow. Suddenly, the bounty hunter's hoverbike jerked to the left, then to the right.

"Hey!" Lobo shouted, trying to regain control of his vehicle. "What's going on?!"

The bike flew up into a somersault and then spun in a corkscrew. Lobo fought with the handlebars, trying to stay on the bike. He became furious when he realized it was the Mechanic's doing.

"Messing with the Main Man's ride?" Lobo asked. "That's just not right!"

"Take me back to Earth," the Mechanic demanded.

GRRR! Lobo growled through gritted teeth. "Not . . . happening." He gripped the handlebars tighter.

"Very well," said the little alien. "You asked for it."

The hoverbike dipped and sped through space. It soon approached the nearest planet, which loomed large before them like a huge, crimson ball.

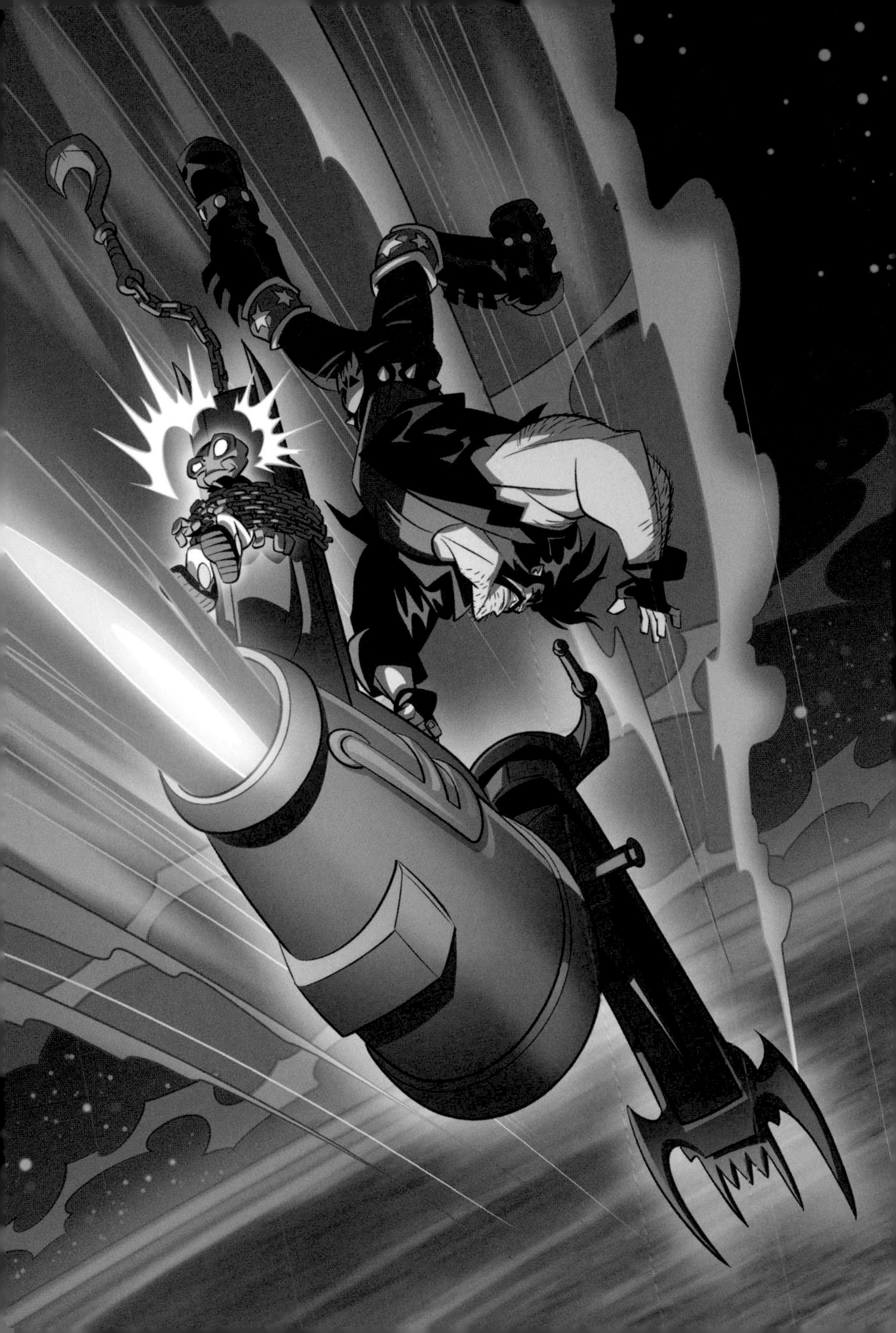

Lobo tried to hit the brakes as the red planet grew closer. But it was no use. They fell faster and faster. The hoverbike punched through the thin atmosphere and raced toward a red desert.

Lobo was able to pull up at the last second before they slammed into the ground. The bounty hunter and his bounty were thrown from the bike amid a giant plume of red sand.

* * *

Superman flew the last oil-rig worker to the lifeboat.

"Thanks, Superman," the crew member said. "Who was that scary guy on the bike?"

The Man of Steel looked up at the sky and let out a sigh. "Someone who thinks he's getting away."

FWOOSH!

Wind rocked the lifeboats as Superman shot up into the clouds. He left Earth's atmosphere and hovered in space. He squinted and glanced around, looking for any sign of the bounty hunter.

"Lobo's bike polluted the sky," Superman said. "Maybe it left a trail out here too."

Using his superpowered vision, the hero quickly spotted a thin trail of pollution snaking off into space. Superman's lips tightened as he took off after the bounty hunter.

The thin trail led all the way to Mars. As he flew closer, Superman scanned the planet's surface for any sign of the bounty hunter. He quickly located a crash site. A long trench stretched across the sand.

Superman spotted Lobo at the end of that trench. The bounty hunter sat on the ground next to a toolbox as he made repairs to his bike. An unconscious Mechanic was tied to the back of it.

Superman lightly touched down next to the scene.

"Hi-ya, Supes," Lobo said without looking up. "Hand me that wrench there, will ya?"

Superman ignored the request and moved toward the Mechanic. The small alien was out cold. The hero scanned him with his X-ray vision but could find no broken bones.

"Gee, thanks for nothing," Lobo said under his breath. He grabbed the wrench himself. "I thought you were supposed to help people."

"Is he all right?" Superman asked.

"Who? Sleeping Beauty over there?" Lobo asked as he put the finishing touches on his bike. "That genius knocked himself out . . . with a crash *he* caused, mind you."

Superman crouched beside the alien. "I'm taking him back to Earth."

Lobo threw the wrench back in the toolbox and stood. "There you go again," he said. "Always with the crazy ideas."

Superman spread his arms wide. "Look around you, Lobo. This is an empty planet. There aren't any innocent bystanders to distract me." He balled his fists. "And I don't have to hold back."

"Yeah, I know." Lobo chuckled as he marched closer. "Sounds like fun," he said just before head-butting the Man of Steel.

WHAM!

The powerful blow drove Superman into the ground like a nail. Only his head and shoulders poked out of the red sand.

Lobo leaned over him. "Now, what were you saying?"

POW!

Superman's fist erupted from the sand, and the bounty hunter was knocked backward. The Man of Steel burst from the ground and flew up to meet Lobo. Not holding back in the least, the hero belted the bounty hunter as hard as he could. Lobo snarled as he was propelled away, disappearing over the horizon.

Superman knew he couldn't hurt Lobo, but maybe that last punch would buy him enough time to get the Mechanic. He flew back toward the hoverbike. Unfortunately, his super-hearing picked up Lobo's whistle.

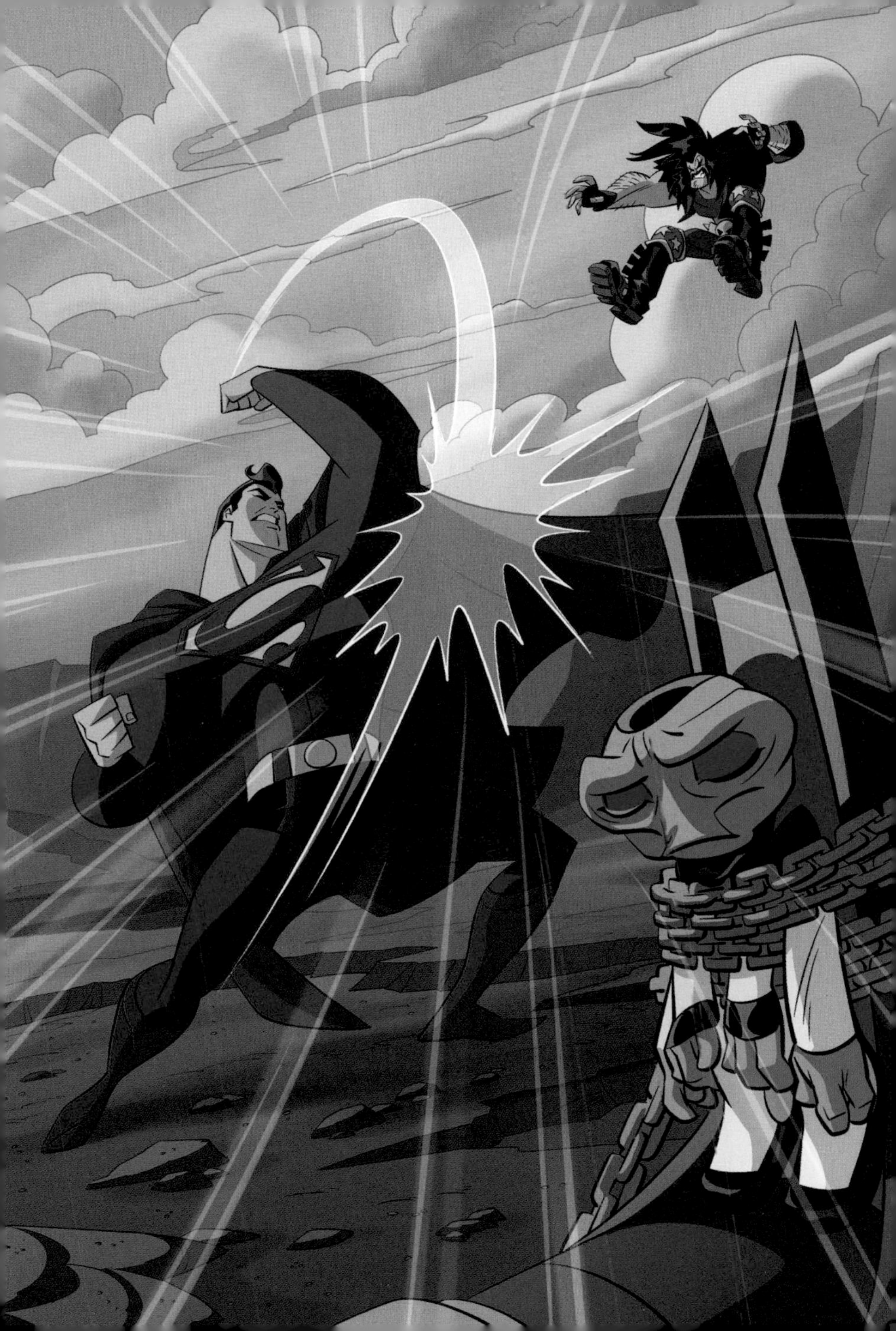

VROOM! VROOM! Before Superman could grab the alien off the bike, the vehicle revved to life and zoomed away.

Superman flew after it as it raced through deep canyons and over steep mountains. The Man of Steel pushed harder, closing in on the bike. He was almost on top of it, reaching out to grab the Mechanic as they flew beneath a thick stone arch.

"Hey, Supes!" yelled Lobo. "Catch!"

Superman glanced up to see the bounty hunter standing atop the arch. He hurled down a boulder the size of a school building. The hero let the bike pull away as he reached up to catch the enormous rock. Superman grunted as he held it aloft long enough for the hoverbike to get clear. Then the boulder slammed to the ground, pinning the hero beneath it.

Lobo laughed as he leaped off the arch and landed next to an even bigger boulder, one the size of a small stadium. The bounty hunter growled as he lifted the huge rock above his head. He carried it a few steps before slamming it onto the first rock. Superman was pinned beneath tons of Martian rock.

Lobo dusted off his hands as his hoverbike pulled up next to him. "And that's why you don't mess with the Main Man!"

He hopped on and revved the engine. Black smoke belched from his tailpipes as he flew away from the planet and into space.

CHAPTER 4

A Fleet of Problems

BOOM!

Superman punched through the last of the boulders and climbed out. Lobo and the Mechanic were nowhere to be found.

"I don't care if he drops a mountain on me," Superman said as he dusted off his uniform. "He is *not* getting away."

The super hero took to the skies, more determined than ever to stop Lobo.

The bounty hunter had been correct about one thing. Superman was supposed to help others. The Mechanic had come all the way to Earth for help. So far, the Man of Steel had let him down. Lobo was just as strong as Superman and couldn't be hurt. So brute force wasn't going to stop him. And so far, Lobo couldn't be reasoned with either.

There has to be some other way to handle this bounty hunter, Superman thought.

The hero followed Lobo's trail away from the planet and out of the solar system. Stars streaked by as Superman hurried to catch up with him.

Luckily, the hero finally found Lobo at a standstill. The bounty hunter sat on his hoverbike surrounded by two different fleets of spaceships. The Mechanic was still out cold on the seat behind him.

"For the last time," Lobo said, "move aside or I start annihilating!"

"We don't take orders from Juran spies," came a voice from the communicator on Lobo's bike.

"Don't be ridiculous! He's not our spy!" said another voice. "He is obviously a Talescian spy. Note the dull features, clear evidence of low intelligence."

Lobo covered his face with both hands. "That's it! I'm blasting everybody!"

Superman raced in front of Lobo and held out his arms. "I think we can all solve this peacefully."

"Oh, hey, Supes," Lobo said with a nod. He pointed to the fleets. "Can you believe these guys? They want to involve the Main Man in their stupid little war."

Superman rounded on the bounty hunter. "Listen, Lobo. You can't solve all your problems with senseless violence."

FUUUUUUSH!

A missile shot from beneath Lobo's hoverbike.

"Sorry, Supes. I wasn't listening," Lobo said with a grin. "I was too busy solving my problem with senseless violence."

Superman sighed and squinted at the missile. Two thin, red beams shot from his eyes and struck the projectile. It exploded harmlessly before reaching the fleet.

"To all Juran ships," shouted a voice from Lobo's communicator. "Half of you fire at the Talescians, the other half at the intruders."

"Prepare to return fire!" ordered the Talescian commander.

Guns from both fleets aimed at each other as well as at Superman and Lobo.

Superman turned to the fleets. "Wait, please!"

Lobo rubbed his hands together. "Now things are about to get interesting."

Superman didn't know what he was going to do. How could he stop everyone, including Lobo, from attacking one another?

Luckily, he didn't have to.

A small, green sphere appeared around him. Two larger ones formed around each of the space fleets. Even Lobo and the unconscious Mechanic floated in their own green spheres. Superman smiled. He recognized those balls of green light.

"Am I interrupting something?" asked a familiar voice. "I hope I am."

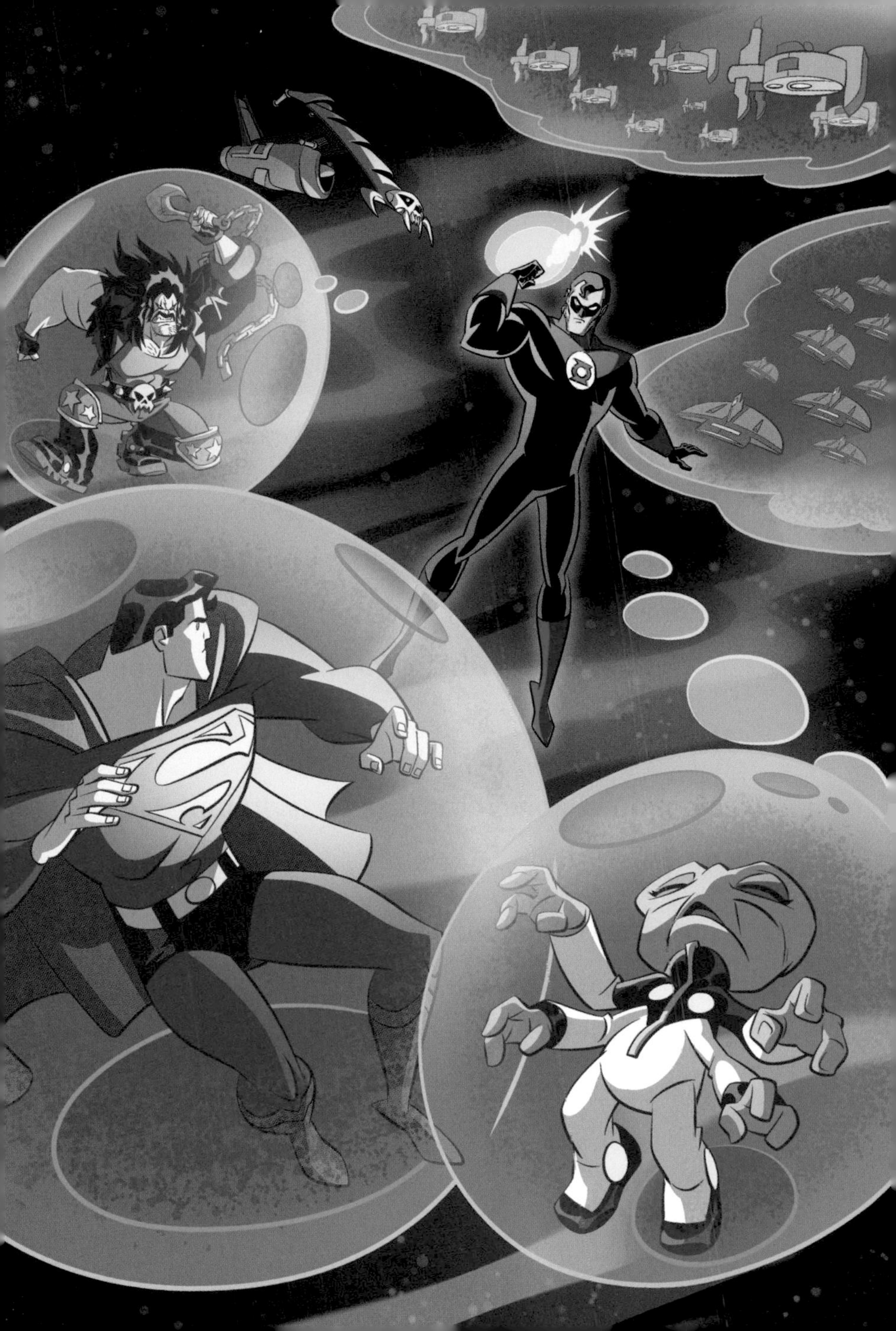

"Lantern Jordan!" shouted the Juran commander. "We didn't know you were nearby."

The Green Lantern, Hal Jordan, floated closer. His power ring glowed as he kept the green spheres in place.

"I'm glad you are," Superman said with a smile. "Good to see you, Hal."

"What are you doing out here, Superman?" Green Lantern asked before glancing at Lobo. "Oh . . . I get it."

Superman nodded at the fleets. "You know these people?"

Hal nodded and sighed. "Yeah, the planets Juray and Talesca are in my space sector," he explained. "As a member of the Green Lantern Corps, I helped them work out a peace treaty a few years ago."

"Which we were following," said the Juran commander. "Until these Talescian spies showed up."

"They're your spies!" the Talescian commander shot back.

"All right, all right," Green Lantern said. "I assure you that none of these people are spies."

"Yeah! The Main Man is not a spy," Lobo agreed. Then he shrugged. "Unless the money's good."

"Please keep to the treaty and return to your planets," Green Lantern continued. "Thank you." He released the ships from their green spheres.

Just then, the guns on all the ships came to life. They swung about and pointed in one direction. All of them were aimed at Lobo.

"We have lost control of the guns!" the Talescian shouted. "This is not our doing!"

Superman had an idea who was behind it. He turned to see that the Mechanic was now wide-awake. His eyes glowed as he floated inside his own protective sphere.

VOOM! TZAP! TZAP! VOOM! VOOM!

Lasers and missiles exploded from every ship. Hal Jordan created a green shield to block the lasers. Meanwhile, Superman flew out and punched every missile he didn't stop with his heat vision.

Lobo hopped on his hoverbike, revved the engine, and flew toward the nearest ship. He loosened his chain and swung it over his head.

"Oh, yeah!" the bounty hunter shouted. "Time for some first-class destruction!"

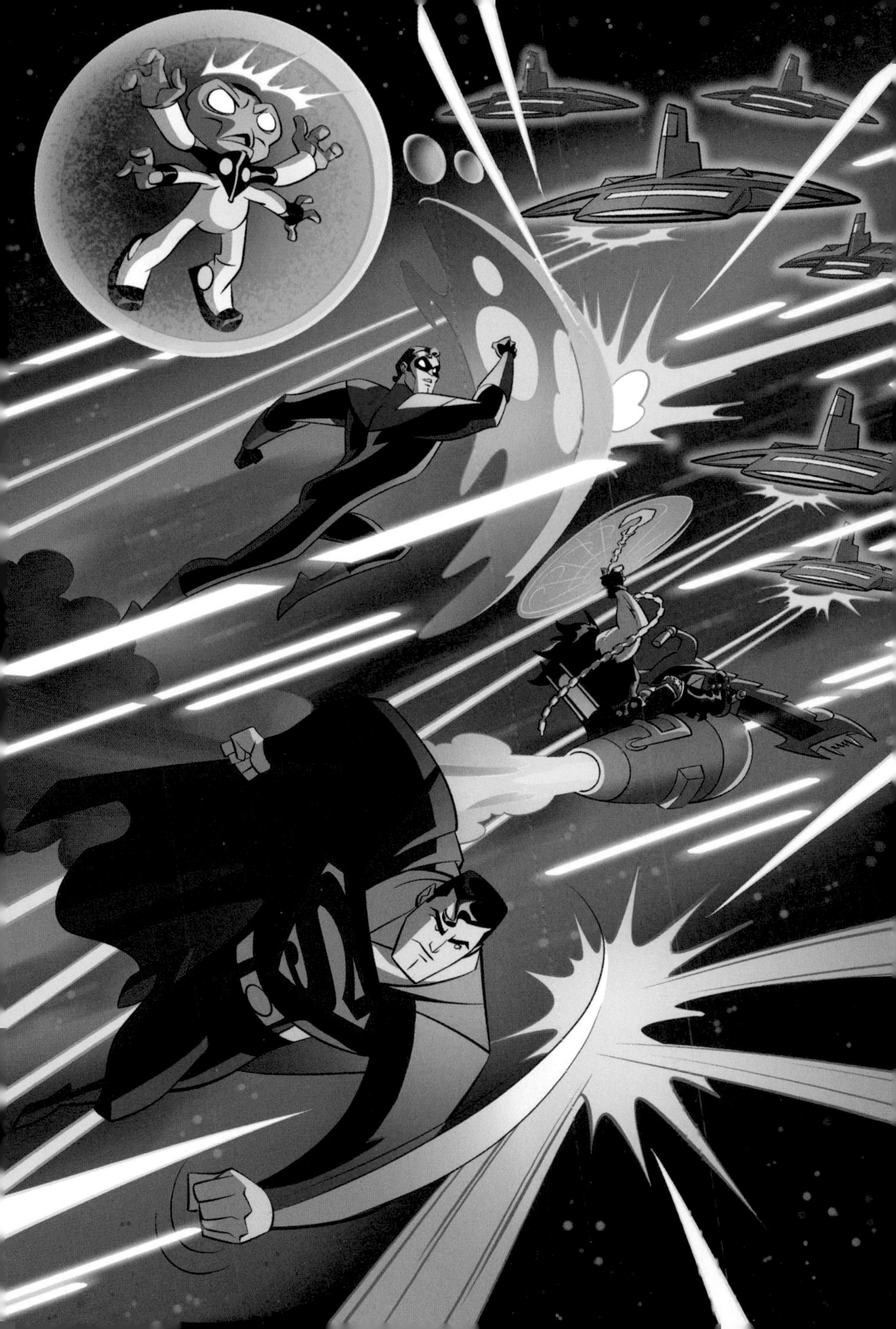

"Lobo!" Superman shouted. "Don't hurt anyone!"

The bounty hunter shook his head. "You're no fun at all." He brought his chain around, merely smashing the guns poking out of the ships.

TZAP! POW! POW! Ka-THOOM!

For a brief moment, Superman, Green Lantern, and Lobo worked together to fend off the attacks. Explosions of every color washed out the stars around them.

I have to convince the Mechanic to stop controlling the ships, Superman thought.

Unfortunately, Lobo beat him to it. While the two heroes were occupied, the bounty hunter drove his hoverbike toward the small alien and punched through the sphere surrounding him.

Superman watched as Lobo pulled a small canister from his belt and flipped a switch. Gas filled the sphere, knocking out the little alien. Lobo threw him over his shoulder and took off.

VROOM!

Once again, Lobo sped away with his bounty.

CHAPTER 5

The Main Man Delivers

With the Mechanic gone, the spaceships stopped firing. Soon after, Green Lantern and Superman destroyed the last of the roving missiles.

"Let me get this straight," Green Lantern said, giving a small wave to the spaceships as they headed back to their home planets. "Are you saying you chased Lobo all the way out here from Earth?"

"That's right," Superman said. The hero explained how the Mechanic came to him for help. "But the trouble is, that bounty hunter and I are so evenly matched. I can barely slow him down."

"I'm sure you'll think of something," Hal told him. He held up his ring. "I come across many challenges, but I can't solve them all with my power ring. Sometimes I have to think of more creative solutions."

"You're probably right," Superman replied. "But I have to catch up to him first."

Hal smiled. "My power ring can help with that." He extended his arm and green light shot from his ring. The light formed into a sleek, one-man spaceship. "This should last long enough for you to find him."

"Thanks," Superman said as he climbed into the ship.

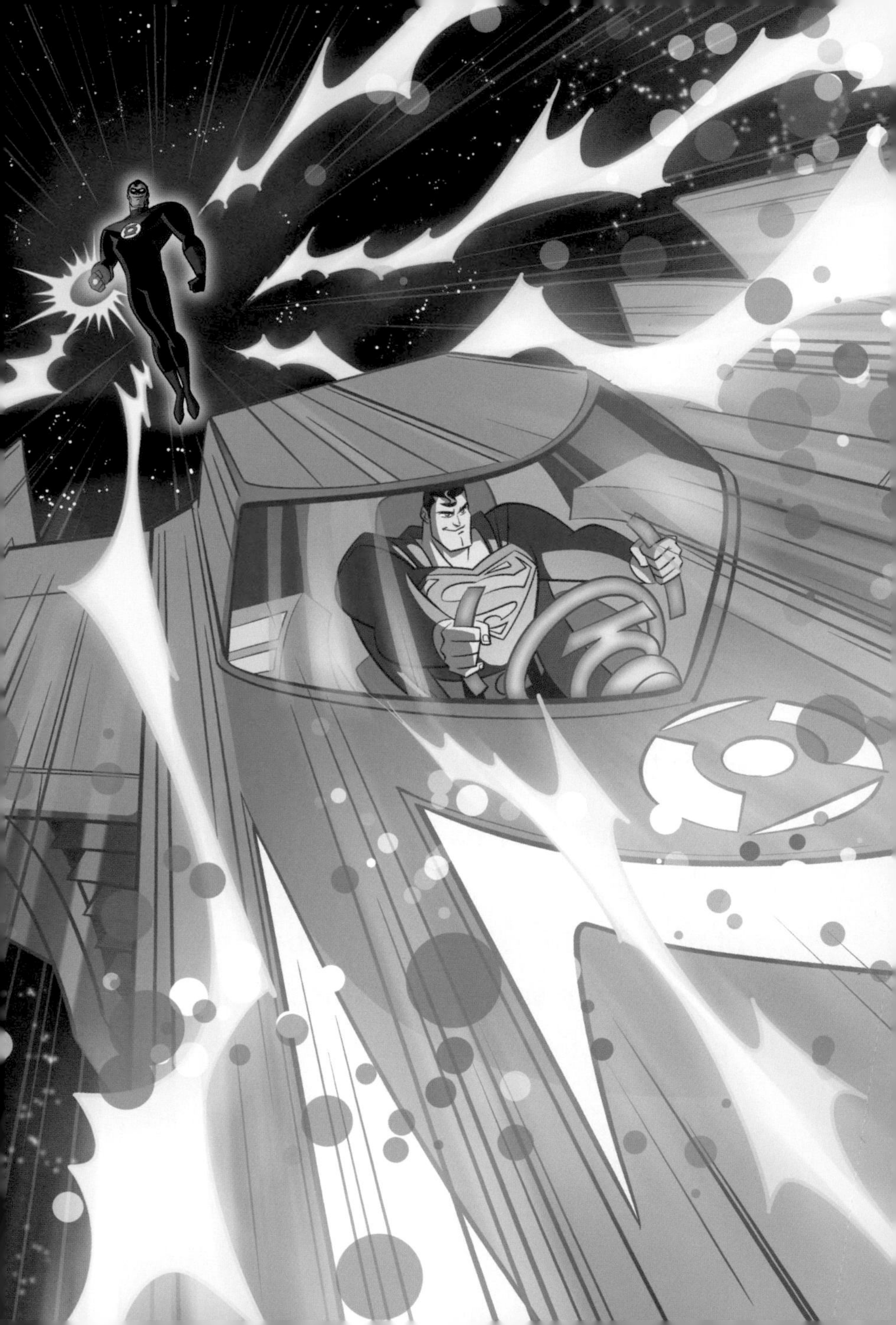

The cockpit hatch closed and Superman gripped the controls. Then the hero was slammed back in his seat as the ship rocketed through space.

Superman concentrated as he steered the craft, still following the hoverbike's trail. Stars streamed past as he moved through space faster than he ever had before. He couldn't help but smile at the thrill of going so swiftly, even for him.

The ship slowed as a huge space station came into view. The base was enormous, but it looked as if it was falling apart. Large structures seemed to barely be attached, while other pieces simply floated beside it.

Nevertheless, Superman spotted Lobo pulling up to it on his hoverbike. The bounty hunter climbed off his bike and floated through an air lock on the side of the station.

I hope I'm not too late, Superman thought.

As he raced closer, the green spaceship around him flickered out of existence. Now he simply flew toward the base and through the air lock.

HSSSSSS!

The door opened and Superman stepped into the corridor. Lobo walked a few feet ahead of him. The unconscious Mechanic was still draped like a sack of potatoes over his shoulder.

"Hold it right there, Lobo," Superman ordered. "This is as far as you go."

Lobo spun around. He dropped the alien and grinned.

"Oh, yeah," the bounty hunter said as he cracked his knuckles. "Big Blue wants another helping."

Lobo ran up to him and threw a punch. Superman blocked the blow, plus three more. His eyes narrowed as he blasted the bounty hunter with heat vision.

FZZZZZ!

Lobo chuckled. "That tickles!"

Superman was worried about damaging the station as they fought. But Lobo wasn't concerned at all. He grabbed the hero by the uniform and slammed him into the metal wall.

WHAM! YANK!

Lobo pulled Superman out of the giant dent and slammed him into the opposite wall. He used the Man of Steel to make holes all down the corridor.

Superman didn't fight back. He had another plan.

"How badly do you want to save your little friend there?" Lobo asked. "Because I can keep wrecking this place." He grinned. "And it doesn't look like it's in great shape to begin with."

"Okay, fine," Superman said. "You win."

The bounty hunter's eyes bulged. "Really? No kidding?" He let go of Superman's uniform.

The Man of Steel smiled. "No, not really."

Superman held up the small canister he had snatched from Lobo's belt. He flicked a switch and a plume of gas shot toward the bounty hunter's face.

TSSSSSSS!

Lobo's eyes widened as he inhaled the gas. "What a . . . dirty trick," he said before passing out and crumpling to the floor.

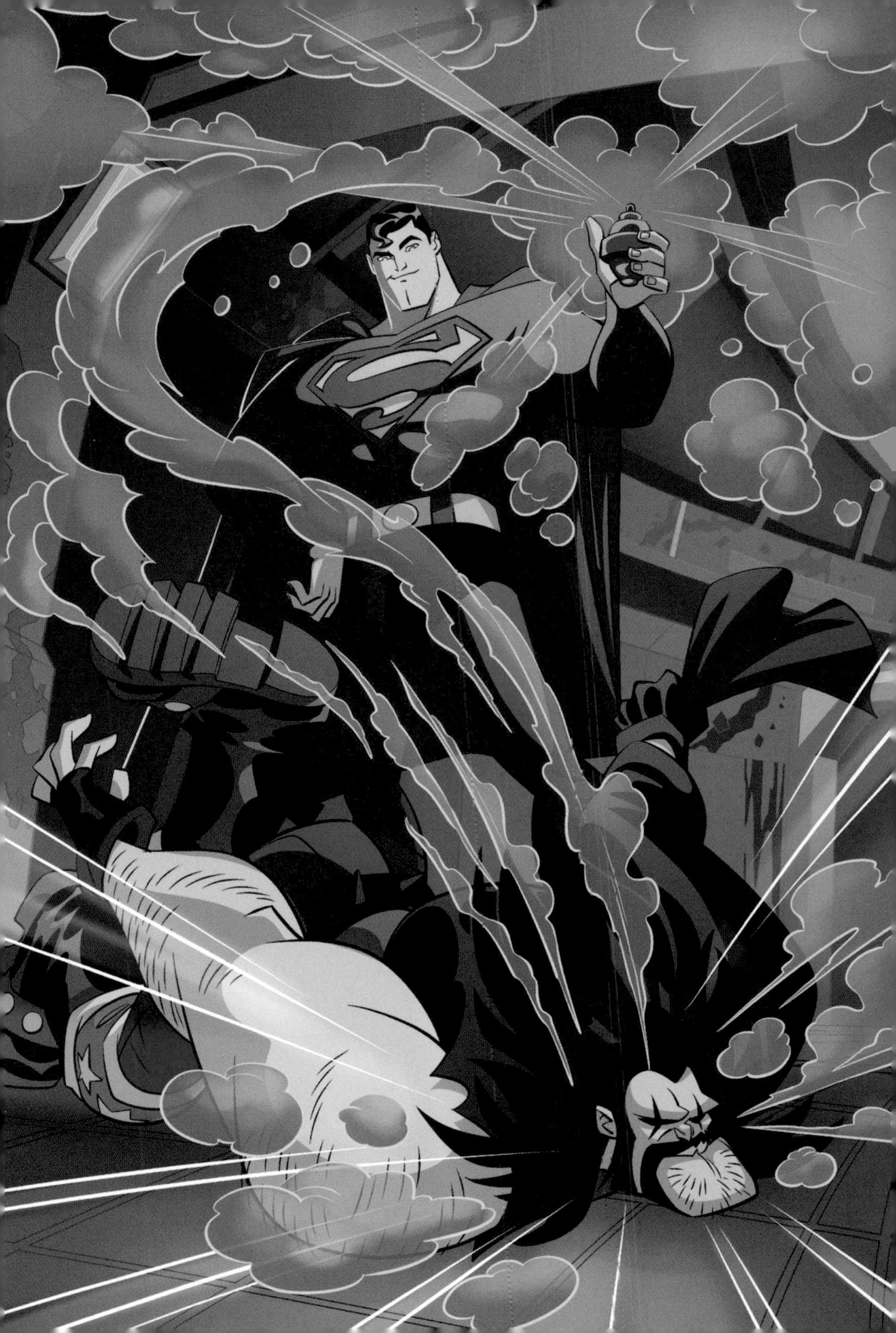

"I learned from the best," Superman said with a smirk.

He stepped over the unconscious bounty hunter and moved toward the Mechanic. The little alien woke up as Superman removed the chain. The Mechanic glanced over at the unconscious bounty hunter. "You did it, Superman," he said. "You saved me."

"Not quite," Superman said. "Now that we're here, let's find out who hired Lobo in the first place."

SHHHHOOP!

A door slid open and two tall, thin aliens stepped through. They had small heads atop long necks with long arms stretching nearly to the floor.

"It is we who hired the bounty hunter to find the Mechanic," said one of the aliens.

The Mechanic hid behind Superman's cape once again.

"We mean you no harm," said the second alien. "We are the Lis-Moorians, and our home, as you can see, is in serious need of repair." The Lis-Moorian lifted one long arm and gestured with a sweeping motion toward the badly damaged corridor.

"Xal Gliknark's reputation is great—but contacting him directly has proved very difficult," the first Lis-Moorian added as she pointed to the Mechanic. "We desperately need his assistance, so we hired Lobo to help us find him."

The tiny alien stepped out from behind Superman. "That's it?" he asked.

The Lis-Moorians nodded. "Only if you agree," they said.

Superman smiled down at the Mechanic. "It looks like you have a chance to help someone now."

A grin stretched across the Mechanic's face as his eyes began to glow. Metal creaked around them as the corridor walls slowly repaired themselves.

Superman's smile faded as deep, groggy laughter echoed in the hallway. Lobo slowly stumbled to his feet. "What did I tell you, Supes?" he said. "The Main Man always delivers."

The first Lis-Moorian handed the bounty hunter a stack of metal bars. "Your payment in full."

Lobo chuckled as he counted them. Then he pushed past Superman as he sauntered toward the air lock.

Superman crossed his arms. "Earth is still off-limits, Lobo."

Lobo waved him away as he reached the hatch. "Don't worry, Supes. The Main Man has no reason to visit that little mud ball of yours." He glanced over his shoulder and grinned. "For now . . ."

Lobo

SPECIES: Czarnian

OCCUPATION: Bounty Hunter

BASE: Mobile

HEIGHT: 7 feet 6 inches

WEIGHT: 640 pounds

EYES: Red

HAIR: Black

POWERS/ABILITIES: Superhuman strength, stamina, and durability. He is also highly skilled at hunting, tracking, and hand-to-hand combat.

BIOGRAPHY:

Lobo is known as the most successful bounty hunter in the entire universe. He always gets his target, even if it means destroying entire planets in pursuit of his prey. In fact, Lobo loves breaking things—and people—so the line of work suits him well. Despite being a self-proclaimed "bad man," Lobo is always true to his word. He will never break his promises, but he does bend them quite often. His employers must choose their words carefully, or they'll end up in a deal they didn't quite bargain for.

- Lobo zooms around from planet to planet atop his trusty, customized hoverbike, the Hog. Since Lobo doesn't need to breathe, he can undergo interstellar travel at super-speed without even wearing a space suit.

- Lobo's accelerated healing abilities allow him to regenerate lost limbs. In fact, Lobo can heal from any injury if he's given enough time.

- Despite his own bad body odor, Lobo has an amazing sense of smell. He is able to sniff out his prey from as far as a galaxy away! He also has the tracking skills of an expert hunter, so hiding from the Main Man is nearly impossible.

BIOGRAPHIES

Author

Michael Anthony Steele has been writing for television, movies, and video games for more than 27 years. He has authored more than 120 books for exciting characters and brands including Batman, Superman, Wonder Woman, Scooby-Doo, LEGO City, Garfield, *Winx Club, Night at the Museum*, and *The Penguins of Madagascar*. Mr. Steele lives on a ranch in Texas, but he enjoys meeting his readers when he visits schools and libraries all across the country. For more information, visit MichaelAnthonySteele.com

Illustrator

Leonel Castellani has worked as a comic artist and illustrator for more than 20 years. Mostly known for his work on licensed art for Warner Bros., DC Comics, Disney, Marvel Entertainment, and Cartoon Network, Leonel has also built a career as a conceptual designer and storyboard artist for video games, movies, and TV. In addition to drawing, Leonel also likes to sculpt and paint. He currently lives in La Plata City, Argentina.

GLOSSARY

annihilate (uh-NYE-uh-late)—to destroy something completely

bounty hunter (BOUN-tee HUN-tur)—someone who tracks and captures others for money

bystander (BYE-stan-dur)—someone who is at a place where something happens to someone else

commander (kuh-MAND-ur)—a person who leads a group of people in a military force

communicator (kuh-MYOO-nuh-kay-tur)—a device that allows people to talk to each other over great distances

derrick (DER-ik)—a tall framework that holds the machines used to drill oil wells

intelligence (in-TEL-uh-jenss)—the ability to learn and understand information

invincible (in-VIN-suh-buhl)—unable to be beaten or defeated

projectile (pruh-JEK-tuhl)—an object, such as a bullet or missile, that is thrown or shot through the air or space

reputation (rep-yuh-TAY-shuhn)—a person's character as judged by other people

unconscious (uhn-KON-shuhss)—not aware; not able to see, feel, or think

DISCUSSION QUESTIONS

1. Superman decides to help the Mechanic without really knowing why Lobo is hunting him. Do you think that was the right decision? Explain your answer.

2. Green Lantern swoops in to help Superman with the standoff in space. Do you think the Man of Steel could have controlled the situation without Green Lantern's help? Why or why not?

3. At the end of the story, we learn the real reason Lobo was hunting the Mechanic. How did that reason change your view of the bounty hunter?